DC COMICS
SUPER HEROES

STORY BY TREY KING
ILLUSTRATED BY
SEAN WANG

SCHOLASTIC

SCHOLASTIC CHILDREN'S BOOKS
EUSTON HOUSE,
24 EVERSHOLT STREET,
LONDON NW1 1DB, UK

A DIVISION OF SCHOLASTIC LTD
LONDON ~ NEW YORK ~ TORONTO ~ SYDNEY ~ AUCKLAND
MEXICO CITY ~ NEW DELHI ~ HONG KONG

THIS BOOK WAS FIRST PUBLISHED IN THE US IN 2015 BY SCHOLASTIC INC.
PUBLISHED IN THE UK BY SCHOLASTIC LTD, 2015

ISBN 978 1407 16341 3

BOOK DESIGN BY ERIN MCMAHON

PRINTED AND BOUND BY L.E.G.O., ITALY

2 4 6 8 10 9 7 5 3 1

WHEN THE WORLD IS IN TROUBLE, IT CAN COUNT ON HEROES TO SAVE THE DAY!

WHEN LEX LUTHOR AND GORILLA GRODD TEAM UP, SO DO SUPERMAN AND BATMAN. THEY WORK TOGETHER TO TAKE DOWN THE VILLAINS AND HELP THOSE IN DANGER.

BETWEEN MISSIONS, THE HEROES HANG OUT AT THEIR SECRET HEADQUARTERS. WHEN THEY AREN'T FIGHTING BAD GUYS, THEY LIKE TO HAVE FUN.

HAS ANYONE SEEN MY BEACH UMBRELLA?

"IF THERE'S AN EMERGENCY, REMEMBER: IT'S NOT ABOUT WORKING FAST, IT'S ABOUT WORKING *SMART!*" SUPERMAN REMINDS THEM.

THE HEROES' MOVIE IS CUT OFF BY A MESSAGE FROM THREE SPACE SUPER-VILLAINS: DARKSEID, SINESTRO AND BRAINIAC. "WE WILL ATTACK YOUR PLANET — UNLESS EVERYONE ON EARTH SENDS US ALL THEIR TOYS. YOU HAVE 24 HOURS!"

ALL OF OUR TOYS?! THOSE VILLAINS!

WORKING TOGETHER, THE THREE HEROES COME UP WITH A VERY SMART PLAN.

YOUR JET IS INVISIBLE!
REMIND ME TO BORROW THE BATWING NEXT TIME . . .
THE THREE HEROES FLY OFF TO OUTER SPACE TO SAVE THEIR FRIENDS, THE WORLD AND – OF COURSE – ALL THE TOYS!

WHEN THE SPACE ALIEN OPENS THE BOX, HE GETS A HERO-SURPRISE. EVERYTHING IS GOING ACCORDING TO THE PLAN.

NEXT, SUPERGIRL PUTS A SHEET OVER HER HEAD AND SNEAKS UP ON SINESTRO. WHEN HE GETS SCARED, HIS RING LOSES POWER.

AFTER THAT, WONDER WOMAN TAKES CARE OF SINESTRO. NOW THE OTHER HEROES ARE FREE. "WHAT A GREAT COSTUME!" SAYS HAWKMAN.

"WHAT A GREAT PLAN!" SAYS GREEN ARROW.

THE HEROES HAVE BEEN SAVED AND THE VILLAINS HAVE ALREADY BEEN DEFEATED. "WAIT A MINUTE," SAYS SUPERGIRL, "WEREN'T THERE *THREE* BAD GUYS?"

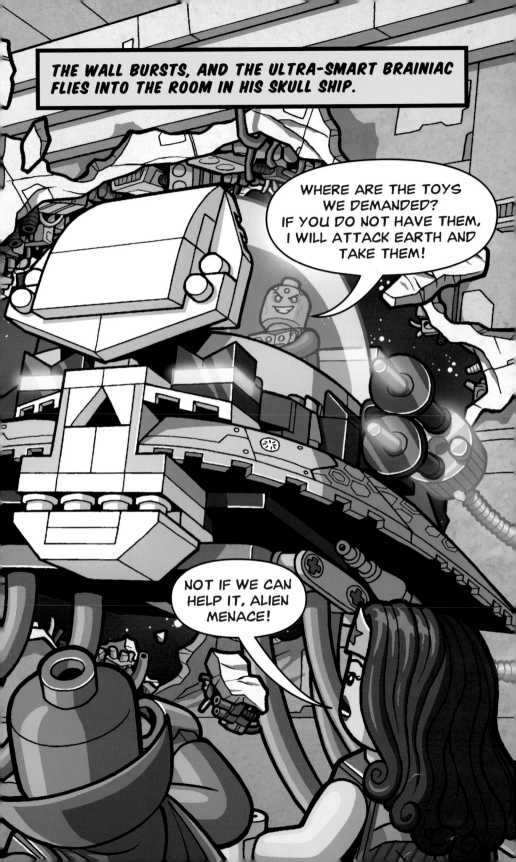

GREEN LANTERN USES HIS POWER RING TO FLY THE VILLAINS TO SPACE JAIL.

"ARE THERE TOYS IN SPACE JAIL?" DARKSEID ASKS. "ONLY IF YOU BEHAVE," GREEN LANTERN ANSWERS.